Spotted tun

Knobby starfish

Siphonalia

Lettered olive

Mutable conch

Scallop

Coquina clam

Calico clam

Tapestry turban

Humphrey wentletrap

Sea urchin

Moon snail

Jewel box

Striped fox conch

Trochus

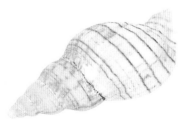

Banded tulip

for mary, who spotted it first

All rights reserved. Published in the United States by
Random House Studio, an imprint of Random House Children's Books,
a division of Penguin Random House LLC, New York.

Random House Studio with colophon is a registered trademark of Penguin Random House LLC.

Visit us on the Web! rhcbooks.com

Educators and librarians, for a variety of teaching tools, visit us at RHTeachersLibrarians.com

Library of Congress Cataloging-in-Publication Data is available upon request.
ISBN 978-0-593-65099-8 (trade) — ISBN 978-0-593-65100-1 (lib. bdg.) — ISBN 978-0-593-65101-8 (ebook)

The artist used ink, watercolor, charcoal, photography, and collage to create the illustrations for this book.
The text of this book is set in 19-point Bell MT Pro.
Interior design by Rachael Cole

MANUFACTURED IN CHINA
10 9 8 7 6 5 4 3 2 1
First Edition

The author wishes to acknowledge Ron Glasser from Jewels of the Sea and
Chandler Olson from Seahorse and Co for their help with shell identification.

IF YOU SPOT a shell

aimée sicuro

RANDOM HOUSE STUDIO · NEW YORK

If you spot a shell

It could be a hiding place for the treasures that you find.

Or a swimming cap for diving into the crashing waves.

You could hide out in the shade on a hot summer's day.

If you spot a shell, it could be your ride,

cruising along a winding trail.

You could listen to the echoes of all the ocean sounds

Or ride a Ferris wheel with friends and go round and round.

It could be a pirate's patch,

a raft that floats,

or a magical kaleidoscope.

If you spot a shell, it could be a kite that flies above the clouds

Or a twisty slide for you to splash down on.

It could be a rocket ship to take you way up high

or a submarine for exploring the wonders of the world below.

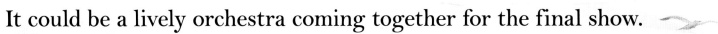

It could be a lively orchestra coming together for the final show.

An ocean serenade to share

with a flock of dancers lifting and spinning into the air.

If you spot a shell, you could imagine most anything.

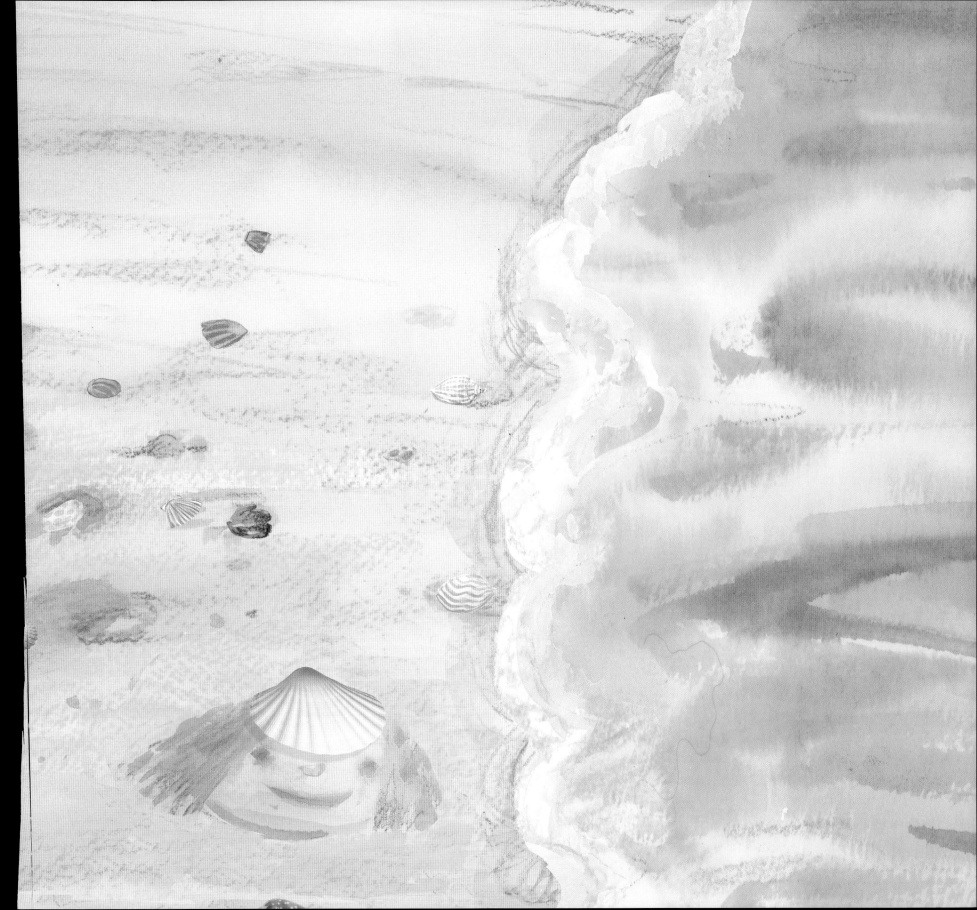

And when the sun is low and the day is done,

we say goodbye to all our beach-time fun.

sand art project

*I*f you're at the beach, you can create your own shell artwork in the sand. All you need is your imagination and some objects you find in nature.

1. Gather shells, rocks, seaweed, twigs, and whatever else you can find.
2. Look at the different shapes and colors of each object. Do they inspire an idea, shape, or image in your mind?
3. Find a nice space to create your art. If your idea requires a flatter surface, you can smooth the area with your hands or the back of a sand shovel.
4. Using a stick or the end of a sand shovel, you can draw an outline of what you want to make.
5. Fill your drawing with the materials you've collected.
6. If you have a camera, take a picture to remember your creation.

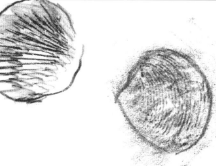

shell rubbings

$\mathscr{A}$ shell rubbing is a great way to capture the patterns and texture of a seashell. For this activity, you will need paper, crayons, and a hard surface like a clipboard or a hardcover book. Using the side of a crayon with the paper peeled off works best. It takes some practice to create a rubbing, and you might need a grown-up's help for the first few.

1. Find a shell with interesting surface texture.

2. Place the shell on the hard surface, and put a piece of paper over the shell.

3. Firmly hold the paper on top of the seashell to keep the shell in place. With the side of your crayon, gently rub the shell until you see the texture revealed on your paper.

4. If you want to capture the outline of the shell, place it on top of your rubbing and trace around it.

5. Then if you want to add more, you can draw a picture around the rubbing. Have fun creating!

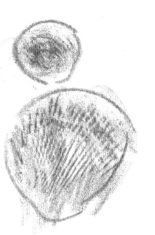

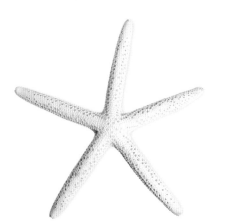

Blue starfish

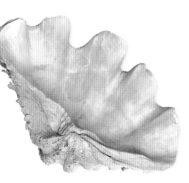

Giant clam

Green limpet

Queen conch

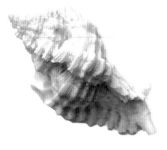

Lace murex

Cockle

Ivory whelk

Scallop

Scallop

Turritella ligar

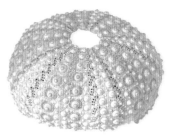

Abalone

Sea urchin

Lightning whelk

Sunrise tellin

Green turban

Veined rapa whelk